Frankie the Makeup Fairy

To Aleka, with lots of love

Special thanks to Rachel Elliot

No part of this publication may be reproduced, stored in a retrieval
system, or transmitted in any form or by any means, electronic,
mechanical, photocopying, recording, or otherwise, without written
permission of the publisher. For information regarding permission,
write to Rainbow Magic Limited c/o HIT Entertainment,
830 South Greenville Avenue, Allen, TX 75002-3320.

ISBN 978-0-545-48480-0

Previously published as *Pop Star Fairies #5: Frankie the Make-up
Fairy* by Orchard U.K. in 2012.

All rights reserved. Published by Scholastic Inc., 557 Broadway, New
York, NY 10012, by arrangement with Rainbow Magic Limited.

SCHOLASTIC and associated logos are trademarks and/or
registered trademarks of Scholastic Inc. RAINBOW MAGIC
is a trademark of Rainbow Magic Limited. Reg. U.S. Patent &
Trademark Office and other countries. HIT and the HIT logo are
trademarks of HIT Entertainment Limited.

12 11 10 9 8 7 6 5 4 3 2 1   13 14 15 16 17 18/0

Printed in the U.S.A.   40

This edition first printing, March 2013

Frankie the Makeup Fairy

by Daisy Meadows

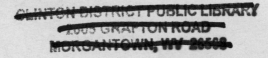

SCHOLASTIC INC.

Fairyland Music Festival

A-OK trailer

Rehearsal tent

Star Village

Picnic hill

Beach ↗

It's about time for the world to see
The legend I was born to be.
The prince of pop, a dazzling star,
My fans will flock from near and far.

But superstar fame is hard to get
Unless I help myself, I bet.
I need a plan, a cunning trick
To make my stage act super-slick.

Seven magic clefs I'll steal —
They'll give me true superstar appeal.
I'll sing and dance, I'll dazzle and shine,
And superstar glory will be mine!

Contents

Makeup Mix-up

The sun was shining on best friends Rachel Walker and Kirsty Tate. It was summer vacation, and they had come to the Rainspell Island Music Festival as special guests of their favorite music group, The Angels.

The girls were standing in the middle of a cluster of activity tents known as

Star Village. There were tents of every shape and color, with fortune-tellers, singing teachers, musicians, and stylists offering their services for free. It was hard to know which one to choose!

"Let's try that one," said Rachel.

She pointed to a tent that sparkled in the morning sun. The sign hanging outside said GLITTER & GO, and people were lining up to have their faces painted.

As the girls joined the line, a group of

teenagers walked past, chatting about the famous people they had seen.

"I heard that Dakota May's here," said one of the boys.

Kirsty and Rachel gasped. Dakota May was one of their favorite superstars.

"I hope she's going to put on a concert while she's here!" said Kirsty.

They started singing Dakota May's latest song, "The Faces of Me," and they only stopped when it was their turn to have their faces painted. Giggling, the girls hurried into the tent and perched on high stools.

"Hi, I'm Chloe," said a bubbly dark-haired girl to Rachel. "What would you like today?"

Rachel knew exactly what she wanted!

"Could I have a rainbow across my cheek?" she asked. "Sure," said Chloe, picking up her jar of makeup brushes. "How about you?" asked the red-haired makeup artist in front of Kirsty. "I'm Dora, by the way."

"I can't decide what I want!" said Kirsty with a smile.

"How about some glittery face paint?" asked Dora. "I can make you shimmer like a fairy!"

Rachel and Kirsty shared a smile. No one else knew that they were

secretly friends
with the fairies.
Rainspell Island
was a very special
place for them,
because this
was where they

had met the fairies for the first time.
Now, in addition to enjoying the
festival, they were helping the fairies
again.

Mean Jack Frost had stolen the
Superstar Fairies' magic music clefs and
brought them to the festival. The clefs
made sure that all aspects of pop music
were a success, but now Jack Frost was
planning to use them to become a
superstar himself!

So far, Kirsty and Rachel had helped
the Superstar Fairies get four of their
magic clefs back from the goblins, who
were hiding them. But there were still
three left to find. Without them, pop
music would be ruined. The girls were
determined not to let that happen!

Just then, a teenage girl with long
blond hair and large sunglasses sat down

on the stool
next to Kirsty.
"Could I have
a butterfly on
my cheek,
please?"
she asked.
Her makeup
artist, Sylvie, started to work. The
teenager glanced over at Rachel.

"That's going to look very cool," she said. "Maybe *I'll* get a rainbow on my face tomorrow."

"Isn't this a fun festival?" said Rachel, smiling back at her. "We've been trying to decide which part we like best, but we can't!"

"I know the feeling," said the girl with a friendly laugh. "I've been coming here for years, and I still can't decide!"

Rachel and Kirsty chatted with the girl about the other festivals she had attended. She seemed to have been to them all! Meanwhile, the makeup artists worked quickly, and when they finished they each held up a mirror in front of the girl they'd been working on. Rachel and Kirsty held their breath, ready to be impressed. But . . .

"Oh," said Kirsty.

"Oh, dear," said Rachel.

Kirsty's green and black face paint

made her look more like
a wicked witch
than a fairy.
Rachel's
rainbow
was a messy
blob of dull
colors, and the
blond girl had
a spooky spider on her cheek instead of a
beautiful butterfly.

The makeup artists all looked
embarrassed, and Sylvie blushed.

"I don't understand," said Dora,
frowning at her makeup brushes.

"We have to stop working," said Chloe. "Something weird's going on."

They left the tent and Rachel and Kirsty gazed at each other unhappily. This was all because of Jack Frost and his goblins!

"Don't be sad," said the teenage girl, looking at their somber faces. "Maybe we can fix it."

As she leaned forward to look at the rainbow on Rachel's cheek, her long blond hair slipped to one side. It was a wig! The girls caught a glimpse of the black bob underneath, and they recognized that hair at once.

"I know who you are," said Rachel in a thrilled whisper. "You're Dakota May!"

Secret Star!

Dakota pulled off her sunglasses and gazed at them pleadingly.

"Please don't say anything," she said. "I'll be mobbed by people wanting autographs, and I just want to hang out at the festival like a normal teenager."

For a moment, Rachel and Kirsty just stared at her in awe. Then a group of

boys and girls
rushed into the
tent, shouting
and squealing.

"Is she in
here?"

"Has anyone
seen her?"

"Where is she?"

"We want
Dakota May!"

"Quick, hide!" said Rachel.
She pointed to a full-length mirror in
the corner, and Dakota darted behind it.
Rachel and Kirsty turned to face the
excited teenagers.

"Dakota May?" said Rachel in a loud
voice. "Didn't I see her go into the dance
tent next door?"

"Or was it the karaoke tent?" Kirsty wondered aloud.

"In any case, I definitely don't see her in here," added Rachel, gazing around.

"Let's go and check out the dance tent!" shouted one of the boys. "Come on!"

The teenagers left the tent, and Dakota stepped out from behind the mirror.

"Are they gone?" she asked. "Thanks, girls! It's great to have so many fans, but sometimes I just want to act like an ordinary girl. Besides, everyone will see me soon — I'm going to be making an appearance at tonight's concert."

Kirsty and Rachel were very excited to hear this

news. They had been planning to go to the concert anyway, but now they were determined not to miss it for the world!

"We're really looking forward to it," said Kirsty. "We love your music."

"That's great to hear!" said Dakota with a winning smile. "I'm just going for a quiet walk first — hopefully without any fans chasing me!"

"We'll keep your secret," Rachel promised with a grin.

Dakota looked
into the mirror
and checked
that her wig
and sunglasses
were on
straight.

"Thanks
again, girls,"
she said,
heading out of the tent. "Maybe I'll see
you at the concert later."

"Definitely!" called Rachel and Kirsty.

As Dakota disappeared from sight,
Rachel noticed something strange. A tiny
glow was coming from a group of
makeup brushes on a table.

"Kirsty!" said Rachel in an excited
whisper. "Look!"

The glow grew brighter, and then
the fattest makeup brush let out a puff
of rainbow-colored
fairy dust. Out of
the sparkling dust
sprang a beautiful
fairy! Her dark,
pixie-style hair
shined in the
light. She
giggled as
she twirled in
midair, shaking
the glittering fairy
dust from her swishy
blue skirt. It was Frankie the Makeup
Fairy!

"Hi, girls," she said. "I came to look
for my clef, but I was hoping I'd find

you, too!" She frowned. "What's the matter with your face paint?"

The girls quickly explained what had happened. Frankie waved her wand and the awful designs disappeared from their faces.

"This is bad," she said. "Some of the best makeup artists in the world are here on Rainspell Island. If they can't create beautiful makeup designs, no one can! It's all because my clef is missing."

"That's what we thought," said Kirsty.

"We have to find your necklace fast," said Rachel in a determined voice. "Let's start by looking around Star Village."

Kirsty held open her shoulder bag, and Frankie slipped inside. They couldn't let anyone see the pretty little fairy!

As Rachel and Kirsty left the Glitter & Go tent, they noticed a long line at the next tent. It definitely hadn't been

that popular earlier, and it was a very boring-looking tent compared to the others. It was pale green, and it was covered in splashes of mud.

"What's going on here?" Rachel asked a boy who was standing in line. "What are you waiting for?"

"It's a face-painting tent," the boy replied. "They're doing the coolest designs ever! I'm going to get a lion on my face!"

Three children were just leaving the tent, and the girls looked at them curiously. Sure enough, they had wonderful designs on their faces — a blue  dolphin, a colorful clown, and a beautiful princess.

"How did they get such amazing makeup when Frankie's magic clef is missing?" asked Rachel.

"I think we should investigate," said Kirsty.

The sign outside the tent was messily painted on an old tin tray:

GREAT GRINS BY GREENY

They peeked into the tent. Inside, a boy was sitting on a low stool. The makeup artist who was about to paint his face was very short, very bald, and very, very *green*.

"It's a goblin!" Kirsty exclaimed.

"And he's wearing my magic clef necklace!" cried Frankie.

Goblin Glamour

"I think your face paint is the best, Greeny!" the boy was saying. "I want to be a green alien like you! Can you give me a long nose and big feet, too? And a necklace just like yours? I want to look exactly like you!"

The boy thought that the goblin's green face was painted on! Greeny muttered

something under his breath and wiped
his makeup brush on his white shirt.

Suddenly, a plan flashed into Rachel's
mind.

"Come with me to the back of the tent,"
she said in a low voice. "I have an idea."

When they were out of sight, Frankie
fluttered out of the bag.

"What's your plan?" she asked eagerly.

"We have to get
into the tent,"
said Rachel.
"Frankie, can
you turn me
into a fairy
and make
Kirsty look
like a superstar?
Then she can

distract the goblin while I try to get the necklace back."

"Great plan!" said Frankie, her eyes sparkling with mischief.

She waved her wand. A flurry of tiny golden mirrors flew from the tip and swirled around Rachel. Instantly, she felt herself shrinking to Frankie's size. Pale pink shimmering wings appeared on her back, and she fluttered them in delight. It felt wonderful to be a fairy again!

"Now it's Kirsty's turn!" she said.

Frankie held her wand high above her head and quickly chanted a magic spell.

"To play a game of 'let's pretend,'
Please glitz and glam my human friend.
This superstar will light the sky,
And turn all heads as she walks by."

She made a circle with her wand, and a stream of sparkling sequins flowed around Kirsty.

After a few seconds, they melted away. Kirsty had been completely transformed into a glamorous superstar!

She was wearing skinny jeans and a loose glittery top. Supercool sunglasses covered her eyes, and her hair was fixed in a spiky, ultra-modern style. Shiny rings covered her fingers, and she carried a large sequined bag on her arm.

"You look fantastic!" said Rachel, clapping her hands together in delight. "This will definitely fool the goblin."

"I feel really tall!" Kirsty giggled, gazing down at her wedge shoes.

She opened her bag to let Frankie and Rachel fly inside. Then she walked around to the front of the tent. The children in the line stared at her in amazement. She could hear their curious whispers.

"Who's that girl?"

"She looks so cool!"

"She must be really famous."

At that moment, the boy with the

 goblin face paint came out of the tent. "Now's your chance!" whispered Frankie, who was peeking out of the bag.

"I can't skip the line," said Kirsty in a low voice.

Frankie gave a little laugh.

"You're a star," she said. "You can do anything you want!"

Kirsty's heart was thumping hard, but she walked forward with confidence, and the line parted to let her through. She strode right into the tent and sat down in front of Greeny the goblin. *Just remember that you're famous*, she told herself. *Be brave!*

Kirsty knew that one of Jack Frost's goblins would be impressed by someone who was proud and rude. She lifted her chin into the air.

"*I* am the most famous star at the festival," she said in a haughty voice. "I heard that *you* are the best makeup artist here. So I'm giving you the honor of making up my face."

Sure enough, Greeny looked thrilled.

"Thank you, Your Starriness . . . Your Coolness . . . Your Famousness," he stammered. "This is a great honor!"

With trembling hands he opened his makeup box, which was filled with jars of colorful face paint and powdery glitter. Rachel and Frankie peeked out of the sequined bag and saw Kirsty point to the clef necklace.

"That's a pretty necklace!" she said. "Aren't you afraid that you'll get makeup all over it? I'd take it off if I were you."

"Anything you say!" said Greeny, gazing adoringly at the famous star.

Rachel and Frankie squeezed each other's hands in glee. The plan was working perfectly!

Rachel in Danger!

"I'll put it somewhere safe," Greeny continued.

The girls hoped that he would put the necklace down on the table, but instead he slipped it into the pocket of his shirt. Rachel flew out of the bag and hovered behind Greeny.

"Distract him!" she mouthed to Kirsty.

If Kirsty could keep him busy, Rachel might be able to take back the necklace without him noticing.

"I want you to tell me all about makeup colors," said Kirsty, looking the goblin straight in the eye. "Which colors should I be wearing?"

"Um . . ." said Greeny, looking confused. "You . . . um . . . bright colors like . . . er . . . green um . . . suit you."

"But what kind of green?" Kirsty demanded.

He just stared at her with wide eyes. He didn't know what to say.

"Show me the kind of green you mean," she ordered.

"Yes, Your Celebrityness," he babbled. "I'll find some!"

As he hunted through his makeup kits, Rachel quietly slipped into his pocket. It was dark in there, and it smelled like dirty socks, but she held her breath and felt around for the necklace. As soon as she had the clef in her hands, she zoomed upward.

But as she flew out of the pocket toward Frankie, there was a loud clap of thunder. With a flash of lightning, someone appeared in the middle of the tent — a person with spiky hair and a very grumpy expression.

"It's Jack Frost!" Frankie gasped in horror. "Quick, Rachel — you have to hide!"

Rachel darted into Greeny's makeup kit with the necklace, as Jack Frost marched up to Greeny with his hands on his hips.

"I've been waiting at the Ice Castle for you!" he roared. "What are you doing here, you silly green goblin? I want the magic clef so I can do my makeup! Where is it?"

Greeny reached into his pocket, and his face fell.

"It's g-g-gone!" he stammered.

Jack Frost looked as if he was going to explode. Even the tips of his spiky hair were shaking with anger.

"You lost my magic clef?" he bellowed. "You worthless fool!"

Just then, something awful happened. Inside the makeup kit, some of the glittery powder went up Rachel's nose. It prickled and tickled, and suddenly there was nothing she could do to stop a massive sneeze.

"ACHOO!"

Greeny and Jack Frost whirled around and saw Rachel in the makeup box with the clef necklace.

"The necklace!" thundered Jack Frost.

"A pesky fairy!" yelped Greeny.

Before anyone else could move, Jack Frost leaped forward and slammed down

the lid of the makeup box, trapping
Rachel inside.

"Gotcha!" he cackled.
"Now I'm taking you
home with me!"
Kirsty jumped
to her feet.
"No!" she cried.
"Bring her back!"
But there was
nothing she could
do! Jack Frost held up
his wand and disappeared in a flash of
icy magic — taking the makeup kit, the
magic clef, *and Rachel* with him!

Greeny gave a growl of rage. He tore
off his shirt, stamped on it, and then
charged out of the tent, yelling at the
line of children who were in his way.

Quickly, Frankie waved her wand. Kirsty's superstar look disappeared as she shrank down to fairy-size.

"We have to rescue Rachel!" Kirsty said, fluttering her wings anxiously.

Frankie nodded. "We're going right after her," she said.

She twirled her wand in the shape of a clef. Fairy dust swirled around them, lifting them into the air. They were on their way.

Inside the box, Rachel had no idea what had just happened. She could feel the box moving, and she could hear someone cackling and muttering.

"I have to see what's going on," Rachel said to herself.

She pushed against the lid as hard as she could. It was very heavy, but she managed to open it a tiny crack and wedge it open with a makeup brush. Now she could hear the voice clearly. It was Jack Frost, and he sounded very pleased with himself.

"I'll show those pesky fairies who's really in charge around here," he said. "No one can stop me now!"

Rachel peeked out through the small opening and gave a gasp of horror.

She was in Fairyland. Jack Frost had brought her to his Ice Castle!

The Glitter Trail

Rachel reached into a makeup jar and scooped out a handful of sparkling pink glitter. Then she pushed it out through the narrow opening in the lid. She felt sure that Kirsty and Frankie would come to find her. When they did, maybe it would help if they had a glittery trail to follow!

Jack Frost carried the kit through the kitchen and up a winding flight of stairs to his bedroom. Through the partly open lid, Rachel saw him gaze at his face in a large mirror with a golden frame.

"I really am a handsome fellow," he said, stroking his chin. "And now, thanks to that silly fairy's clef, I'll look even better!" Rachel darted backward as he opened the lid above her. "I'll take that," said Jack Frost, seizing the magic clef necklace.

He placed it around his neck, and
looked into the mirror.

"It looks good on me, don't you agree?"
he said.

Rachel decided to play along with
him. After all, Frankie and Kirsty might
already be in the castle,
looking for her.
She had to keep
Jack Frost
talking, and
she had to
stay close
to the clef.

"Oh, yes,"
she said. "It
makes you
look very . . .
um . . . magical."

"Pass me that brush," Jack Frost ordered. "And that jar of blue powder there. And the silver glitter. Quickly!"

Rachel did as she was told. She watched as Jack Frost began to paint a beautiful icy blue lightning bolt across his face. Where were Frankie and Kirsty — and would they find her glitter trail in time?

Kirsty felt a chill on her arms and legs, and then realized with delight that Frankie had transported them from Greeny's makeup tent all the way to the courtyard of Jack Frost's Ice Castle.

Kirsty blinked the fairy dust out of her eyes. There was no sign of Jack Frost or of Rachel. But her eagle eyes noticed something pink shimmering on the cold flagstones.

"Look, Frankie — makeup!" she said. "Let's follow it!"

They flew quickly, keeping their eyes on the glittery trail. But when it led them into the kitchen, they were dazzled! The room was full of shiny metal bowls, polished chrome handles, mirrored cupboards, and gleaming pots and pans. The glittery trail was reflected back at the fairies hundreds of thousands of times.

"I can't tell which is the real trail and which is a reflection!" cried Kirsty, rubbing her eyes.

"Keep your eyes on the ground," said Frankie. "Don't look up!"

They flew so close to the ground that their knees brushed against the floor tiles, and they found the real trail again. The two fairies followed it out of the kitchen and up to Jack Frost's bedroom. The door was open, and they peeked inside. Rachel was flitting around Jack Frost, handing him makeup brushes and powders. He was squinting into the mirror,

painting icicles on his eyelids. There wasn't an easy way of getting the clef back now that it was hanging around his neck. But the reflections in the kitchen had given

Kirsty an idea. "Have you ever seen a fun house mirror?" she asked Frankie. "Could your magic make Jack Frost think that his makeup looks terrible?"

Frankie gave a sly grin and nodded. Together, they flew into the room and hid behind the mirror. Rachel was hovering close by, and her face lit up when she saw them.

"Rachel, can you get Jack Frost to close his eyes?" Kirsty whispered.

Rachel nodded and fluttered closer to Jack Frost, who was just finishing the last icicle.

"Those look wonderful," said Rachel. "Maybe you should close your eyes to let them dry properly. It would be a shame if you smudged them after all your hard work."

"You're right," said Jack Frost, closing his eyes at once. "My makeup has to be perfect!"

Frankie darted out from behind the mirror and swished her wand across the surface. It rippled like water on a pond,

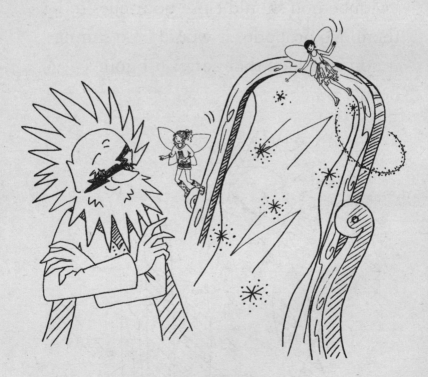

and then Frankie flew out of sight again.

"You can open your eyes now," said Rachel.

Jack Frost opened his eyes and looked into the mirror. . . .

Wibble-Wobble

Jack Frost made a strange croaking noise in his throat.

"What — is — *that*?" he choked.

Frankie had transformed his mirror into wibbly-wobbly fun house glass! The mirror showed a tiny head with an enormous chin, all smeared in blue and silver.

"I look ridiculous!" he screeched. "What's wrong with that fairy necklace?"

"Maybe the clef's magic works differently for you," said Rachel quickly. "You should probably let me have it back after all!"

"No chance!" bellowed Jack Frost.

"It's MINE!" He stomped around the bedroom in anger, and Rachel darted behind the mirror. She hugged Kirsty and Frankie.

"Thank you for coming to rescue me!" she said. "But how are we going to get the magic clef back now?"

"Making him look terrible didn't work," said Kirsty thoughtfully. "I wonder what would happen if Frankie fixed the mirror."

"It's worth a try," said Frankie, tapping the mirror with her wand. Rachel fluttered up and perched on top of the mirror frame. Jack Frost was still stomping around, kicking pieces of furniture and scowling.

"Why don't you take another look?" Rachel suggested. "Maybe it's not as bad as you think."

"Don't be ridiculous!" roared Jack Frost.

But as he glared at her, he caught a glimpse of himself in the mirror. This time, the reflection was perfect. Jack Frost's mouth fell open. Thanks to the magic clef necklace, he had never looked so good!

Enchanted by his own face, Jack Frost  moved closer to the mirror. He couldn't take his eyes off his own reflection. Slowly, Frankie and Kirsty slipped out from behind the mirror.

They fluttered behind Jack Frost and carefully unhooked the necklace. Staring dreamily at his reflection, Jack Frost didn't notice a thing as they pulled the magic clef from his neck.

As soon as it was in Frankie's hands, it shrank to fairy-size.

"So handsome . . ." murmured Jack Frost, turning his face so he could see both sides.

"Let's get back to Rainspell Island!" whispered Frankie.

With a wave of her wand, the three friends disappeared, leaving Jack Frost alone . . . but very happy!

That evening on Rainspell Island, fans were in for a treat. Dakota May was about to give her performance, and Rachel and Kirsty were standing in the front row.

"Thank goodness everyone's makeup is back to normal," said Rachel. "We can really relax and celebrate now."

She had a brightly colored rainbow painted on her cheek and Kirsty's face was sparkling with fairy glitter. The designs had been conjured up by Frankie, who was hidden beneath Kirsty's hair so that she could enjoy the concert, too.

"But Jack Frost still has two of the clefs," said Kirsty with a sigh. "There are still two more Superstar Fairies who need our help. I hope this concert will go all right while those two necklaces are missing."

"My clef will provide just enough magic for this performance to turn out perfectly," said Frankie. "I know you'll help Alyssa and Cassie just like you've helped me . . . but right now, it's time to dance!"

The crowd went crazy as Dakota May bounced onto the stage. She looked completely different than she had earlier. She had her familiar shiny black bob instead of the long blond wig, and her perfect makeup made her glow. But what really lit up the stage was her big, beaming smile.

"Welcome to Rainspell Island, everyone!" she said. "This is a place that's all about friendship and helping one another. I'd like to dedicate the next song to two girls who helped me today. They know who they are!"

Frankie, Kirsty, and Rachel cheered as the music started and Dakota's clear, beautiful voice soared out across the cheering crowd. It was the girls' favorite song — "The Faces of Me."

"It might seem that I have different faces,
For different people and different places.
But in my heart I'm still me,
That's who I will always be."

Kirsty and Rachel shared a happy smile. The music festival was still in danger, and they were facing more exciting adventures. But just for this evening, they were going to dance and enjoy the music — just like everyone else!

RAINBOW magic™

THE SUPERSTAR FAIRIES

Frankie has her magic clef back.
Now Kirsty and Rachel need to help

Alyssa
the Star-spotter Fairy!

Read on for a special sneak peek. . . .

Showers and Sparkles

"Another gorgeous morning at the Rainspell Island Music Festival!" said Kirsty Tate happily. "Do you think I should wear this daisy headband today, Rachel?"

Her best friend, Rachel Walker, looked at their reflections in the big bathroom mirror.

"Definitely!" she said with a smile.
"The white petals look so pretty against
your dark hair."

The girls had just finished showering
and getting dressed. They were camping
at the festival with Rachel's parents, and
they were all special guests of The Angels
music group.

"I think you should wear my rose
headband," Kirsty said, handing it to
Rachel. "It will look great on you."

"I feel so lucky to be here," said Rachel
as she arranged the headband in her
hair. "I've lost count of all the amazing
things we've done — and the fabulous
concerts we've been to!"

"Plus the fun we've had helping the
fairies," said Kirsty with a twinkle in
her eye.

No one knew that the girls were friends with the fairies of Fairyland. They had often helped the fairies outwit grumpy Jack Frost and his mischievous goblins. Soon after they had arrived on Rainspell Island, they met the Superstar Fairies, who used their magic clef necklaces to keep pop music sounding great. Jack Frost and his goblins had stolen the clefs and brought them to the festival to help Jack Frost become a superstar. So far, Kirsty and Rachel had helped five of the Superstar Fairies find their magic clefs.

"I just hope that we can find the final two missing necklaces before the end of the festival," said Rachel.

"Me, too," said Kirsty. "It would be terrible if Jack Frost managed to ruin it for everyone. There are still lots of fantastic concerts to look forward to."

"Yes, I can't wait to see Jacob Bright at the Talent of Tomorrow show later," said Rachel. "He's one of the biggest up-and-coming stars here."

"And we still haven't seen Jax Tempo perform," said Kirsty. "I wonder when he'll be onstage. He must be very good to get so famous so quickly — I hadn't even heard of him until the festival started."

"Well, I'm ready to go," said Rachel. "Let's get our things and head back to the tent."

Kirsty put her hairbrush and spare headbands back into her bathroom caddy while Rachel went into the shower stall to get her shampoo. But as she leaned

over the shower drain, she noticed that
the remaining bubbles were sparkling
with rainbow colors.

Rachel felt a tingle of excitement
running up and down her spine. . . .

RAINBOW magic™

SPECIAL EDITION

Three Books in Each One—
More Rainbow Magic Fun!

Joy the Summer Vacation Fairy
Holly the Christmas Fairy
Kylie the Carnival Fairy
Stella the Star Fairy
Shannon the Ocean Fairy
Trixie the Halloween Fairy
Gabriella the Snow Kingdom Fairy
Juliet the Valentine Fairy
Mia the Bridesmaid Fairy
Flora the Dress-Up Fairy
Paige the Christmas Play Fairy
Emma the Easter Fairy
Cara the Camp Fairy
Destiny the Rock Star Fairy
Belle the Birthday Fairy
Olympia the Games Fairy
Selena the Sleepover Fairy
Cheryl the Christmas Tree Fairy
Florence the Friendship Fairy
Lindsay the Luck Fairy

📖 SCHOLASTIC

scholastic.com
rainbowmagiconline.com

RAINBOW magic™

There's Magic in Every Series!

The Rainbow Fairies
The Weather Fairies
The Jewel Fairies
The Pet Fairies
The Fun Day Fairies
The Petal Fairies
The Dance Fairies
The Music Fairies
The Sports Fairies
The Party Fairies
The Ocean Fairies
The Night Fairies
The Magical Animal Fairies
The Princess Fairies
The Superstar Fairies

Read them all!

scholastic.com
rainbowmagiconline.com